THE PASSION OF ST. MARIA GORETTI

A DRAMA IN THREE ACTS

BRYAN DE JUSTIN

ISBN: 979-8-9987581-8-8

Bryan de Justin

Writing

Giulia Martini

Illustration

Dedication

To Melissa Gisselle Jimenez, Melinna Lissette Hofmann, and Vincent Alexander Jimenez

My siblings, with love, hope, and faith.

Other Plays by Bryan de Justin

The Centurion of Capernaum

Anesidora: A Dramatic Poem

The Descent of Orpheus

Lilith, Adam & Eve

The Conflict of Snow White: An Occult Drama

THE PASSION OF ST. MARIA GORETTI

A DRAMA IN THREE ACTS

BRYAN DE JUSTIN

PERSONS

MARIA GORETTI

ASSUNTA GORETTI, *Maria's mother*

LUIGI GORETTI, *Maria's father*

ANGELO, *Maria's older brother*

MARIANO, *Maria's younger brother*

SANDRINO, *Maria's youngest brother*

ERSILIA, *Maria's younger sister*

TERESA, *Maria's second youngest sister*

GIOVANNI SERENELLI, *Friend, colabourer, and cohabitant of Luigi*

ALESSANDRO SERENELLI, *Son of Giovanni, Maria's admirer*

FATHER RAFFAELO, *Priest*

DOCTORS & NURSES

CARABINIERI

The events transpire in The Kingdom of Italy during the reign of King Umberto I and King Victor Emmanuel III. The characters speak in Italian.

TABLE OF CONTENTS

ACT I

SCENE I

The farmhouse of Luigi Goretti in Le Ferriere. It is the early dawn of the 27th of April, 1900. In a chamber, there lieth asleep the children of Luigi and Assunta Goretti close together. Angelo, Mariano, and Sandrino lay asleep together on a pallet. Maria, nine years of age, and Ersilia lay in another. The infant Teresa sleepeth betwixt Assunta and Luigi, beneath her arm. The cock crows loudly. Assunta exclaims and rises, awakening from a nightmare and breathing heavily.

ASSUNTA

– *whispering in an urgent tone.* – Husband, awaken, hear me! You must hear my words! Oh, husband, the sun has begun to rise, but before it finds us, you must hear me.

LUIGI

– *partly asleep.* – What has happened?

ASSUNTA

My dreams have been plagued by fearful signs and visions. Oh, even now, it is as though I see them yet before my eyes!

LUIGI

– *more alert, slightly irritated.* – Woman, why do you distress yourself and me with such things? Do you not see the celestine sky, how it becomes more azure with the approach of the sun? The day draws near, and you concern yourself with dreams?

ASSUNTA

– *turning towards her husband, still distressed.* – If you had dreamt the dream I have dreamt this night, you would feel as I do now. I have dreamt of the Virgin of Sorrows! She came near to me with such loud tears that to see her was to feel the sorrow of the world. Impelled by compassion, I knelt down and began to pray. She looked at me and wiped a tear from her beautiful face with her dark mantle. As she approached, she took her sorrowful, impaled heart from her chest and placed it into mine. After she did this, her sorrow and mine were one. I was made to understand that she was not weeping for herself or her Son, rather for me. After she had done this, my first thought was of you.

[Assunta places her hand firmly on his chest. He opens his eyes and beholds her.]

ASSUNTA
I implore you, husband, do not tend the fields this day, for I fear some ill fate may fall upon you.

[Luigi lifts her hand from his chest and places it on the bed. He rises from the bed and stands.]

LUIGI
You know well that a day absent from work is calamitous. Spring approaches, and with it, its fruits.

[He prepares his shoes beside the bed. Assunta stands and walks before him.]

ASSUNTA
– *more anxious and louder than she realises.* – Surely a day or so of hunger weighs lightly against the evasion of destruction and despair! Oh, husband, do not go hence into the fields! Stay, stay or you shall kill your wife of worry!

[Maria stirs, and moans gently.]

MARIA
– *partly asleep.* – Mama...

[Luigi looks at Assunta seriously. Assunta turns and walks to Maria, placing a kiss on her forehead and her hand on Maria's cheek.]

ASSUNTA

– *tenderly.* – Have I awoken you abruptly?

[Maria gives another gentle moan of denial.]

ASSUNTA

– *still tenderly.* – Daughter, awaken. The day approaches, and the duties are many.

[Maria gradually rises from her sleep. Assunta turns to awaken the eleven-year-old Angelo. Luigi stops her midway.]

LUIGI

– *speaking gently, yet audibly.* – Do not awaken him today. The day's duties are enough for me alone. *(Admittingly.)* And if your dream of the Virgin indeed bore a sign, as do the dreams of early morning, it would be best that my sons and daughters remain preserved from harm and sheltered. In the meantime, let Maria assist you with the others.

[Luigi leaves. Maria and Assunta commence their household duties.]

SCENE 2

Later that same afternoon. In the dwelling of Luigi and Assunta. Assunta is nursing Teresa. Angelo plays with a stick. Maria sews nearby. Assunta bounces her leg, despondent, still pensive regarding her dream.

A VOICE WITHOUT

– *urgently.* – Maria! We enter and bring you your husband!

[Rapidly, she turns herself around and covers her chest. The door bursts open. Enter Giovanni and Alessandro, carrying Luigi, barely conscious, on their shoulders. Upon seeing this, Assunta places Teresa on the pallet and rises, motioning for them to place Luigi on their bed.]

ASSUNTA

– *nervously.* – What has occurred?

GIOVANNI

– *straining.* – Your husband, Assunta, one moment spoke and laboured with us, but the next, collapsed on the soil. Thankfully, Alessandro was beside him to interrupt his fall.

[Assunta grabs Luigi frantically by the wrist]

ASSUNTA

– *worried.* – His flesh is temperate. He has fever.

GIOVANNI

– *sincerely.* – Yes, I noticed that as well.

[Assunta gazes at Giovanni seriously]

ALESSANDRO

– *in an empathetic, calming tone.* – It was for that reason I called for someone to fetch a doctor. They should arrive in due time.

[Maria approaches from the background behind Alessandro and beholds her father. Alessandro gazes sympathetically at her.]

ALESSANDRO

– *tenderly.* – Be not afraid, little lamb. *(Removing her hair from her shoulders gently and placing his hand on her back.)* He has only need of water and sustenance. *(With reassurance, appealing to her naïvete.)* Surely, it is only due to weariness.

MARIA

– *softly, searching his eyes.* – But he has never fallen before.

[She places her hand gently in Alessandro's. Alessandro lovingly clutches it. Maria turns to behold her father.]

ALESSANDRO

No, but we are all men, not stone. *(Turning to Assunta.)* I have sent Paolo for a doctor. He should return soon.

[Assunta hears, but does not acknowledge, still transfixed by her husband's condition. A thousand thoughts cross her mind. Maria moves slowly toward the bedside. Alessandro stands nearby, hands clasped behind his back, as though reluctant to leave. He watches Maria with concern. Assunta begins weeping. Maria soon does as well. Alessandro embraces Maria protectively.]

ASSUNTA

– *weeping.* – What shall become of me if harm befalls you, husband!

[A knock is heard. Giovanni opens the door hastily. A tall man in dark garments and carrying a dusty satchel enters quietly–it is a Doctor. He speaks with soft authority.]

DOCTOR

– *solemnly.* – God be with you. *(Examining the room.)* Make room. Let the air pass. I must see him.

[The family parts. The doctor kneels at Luigi's side, inspecting his eyes, breath, and limbs. He places his palm upon Luigi's brow.]

DOCTOR

The fever is not ordinary. When word reached me, I had prayed it to be merely a blast of a malign African wind. Yet even now, his blood swells as the marshland. *(He beholds Assunta and her children before inhaling solemnly.)* It is the breath of the mosquito. He has been struck with malaria.

[A grave and heavy silence.]

ASSUNTA

– *in disbelief.* – It cannot be... the fields have been dry, the wind has been strong, there has been no still water!

DOCTOR

– *sympathetically, but with difficulty.* – It takes only one pool of stillness.

[He removes a vial of quinine from his bag and prepares to administer it.]

DOCTOR

If the Virgin be gracious, and the medicine swift, we may yet drive it from him. But I do not promise it. It shall require medicine and prayer.

[He places the vial in Assunta's hands.]

DOCTOR

A spoon every three hours. And prayer, night and day.

[He looks solemnly at Maria, then at the children, now quiet and watching. He departs. Luigi moans, half-unconscious. Assunta bends over him. He opens his eyes slowly.]

LUIGI

– *weakly.* – The sky... it is strange...

ASSUNTA

I am here. The children are safe. Rest, my heart. Rest.

LUIGI

– *delirious.* – I see a coldness canopy the fields... A shadow falls upon this house this very hour.

[He shivers violently. Assunta clutches his hand and looks to Maria.]

ASSUNTA

Maria, daughter, fetch the old candle from the kitchen, and the rosary. We shall begin a novena to the Queen of Virgins.

[Maria nods and exits swiftly. Alessandro, still standing behind, watches her go. He clasps his hands behind his back, his brows furrowed in something like worry. Giovanni places a hand on Alessandro's shoulder, and speaks lowly.]

GIOVANNI

– *quietly.* – Come. Let us give them their peace.

[They exit. Maria returns with the rosary and candle. The family gathers, lit only by the flicker of candlelight. Assunta kneels at the bedside, the baby Teresa stirring faintly nearby. Maria's voice is calm and solemn as she begins praying:]

MARIA

O Mary, Queen of Virgins... pray for us.

CHILDREN

– *softly, in imperfect unison.* – Pray for us.

ASSUNTA

O Mary, Virgin most powerful...

ALL

Pray for us.

MARIA

O Mary, Virgin of Virgins...

ALL

Pray for us.

[The prayers of the Sorrowful Mysteries continue. Outside, the wind shifts. Night falls. All is silent upon the land.]

SCENE 3

Three days have passed since Luigi was struck with fever. It is the third day of the novena to the Queen of Virgins. The sun is veiled by grey rain clouds. Maria kneels alone in the courtyard, washing her father's garments in a bucket of water. The basin ripples with the wind, which comes and goes in sighs. The stain of dirt and blood does not lift. She scrubs silently. Her mouth is closed in prayer, though no words issue forth. Then, a sound behind her – footsteps in the dust. Alessandro, eighteen years of age, enters. She perceives him in the reflection of the water.

ALESSANDRO

– *gently, as if afraid to disturb her stillness.* – Maria, forgive me if I disturb you.

[She turns not, but gazes into his reflection with sorrowful eyes, far beyond her years.]

ALESSANDRO

– *childlike.* – Little lamb, will you not greet me? It has been three days since I last heard your voice. *(Drawing near.)* I have felt your sorrow so closely, it has become my own.

MARIA

There is no need for smiles, Alessandro. From where will I find them? Moreover, we are in prayer to the Virgin of Sorrows. We must mourn with her.

ALESSANDRO

Even so... (*Touching her chin lightly and drawing it toward him.)* Could you not spare a smile for me?

(He pulls out several violets he had concealed and offers them to Maria. She turns away. She wrings out the cloth and lays it over a thread.)

ALESSANDRO

– *overcome with a quiet intensity.* – Would it not be sweet, in these dark hours, to share some warmth? Even a brief kindness. A hug, perhaps... or a kiss?

[She washes another cloth, still perceiving Alessandro in the reflection of the water.]

MARIA

– *sincerely.* – Alessandro, though I love you, my heart has no strength for hugs and kisses.

ALESSANDRO

– *with quiet desperation.* – Maria, will you not embrace me then, even briefly?

MARIA

– *uncomfortable.* – Alessandro, I must continue washing.

[A silence. She lifts the next garment and lays it in the water. Alessandro falters, watching her. He steps closer, his voice trembling with a strange mixture of desire and desperation.]

ALESSANDRO

You are so small... and yet you possess a soul far older than the wisest of men. Your hands work as a father's do. Your voice is gentle, as a dove in the orchard. Your words have always seemed older than your years. You are an angel who has taken the human form of a little girl.

[He reaches out, as if to touch her hair again, but she shrugs him off, irritated. Her eyes meet his directly for the first time.]

MARIA

– *sternly.* – Alessandro, let me wash in peace.

[Alessandro is shocked and taken aback.]

ALESSANDRO

– *quietly desperate, hurt.* – But I love you.

MARIA

As I love you, but leave me in peace.

ALESSANDRO

– *with a trembling voice.* – Then I shall remain beside you silently, if only you will speak sweetly to me. Let me walk beside you when you fetch the water. Let me touch your hand without you pulling away.

[A silence falls between them. Maria is visibly bothered. Alessandro gazes at her with eyes of concern.]

ALESSANDRO

– *strongly.* – I would never hurt you... but when you look at me as though I am dust beneath your feet – *(tears begin to well)* – when you ignore me as though I were no more than a broken wall or the beasts that peck the earth, then my heart breaks.

[She does not reply. She bends and lifts the basin. He watches her in silence. Then, with a sudden pain in his voice:]

ALESSANDRO

Why do you wound me so, Maria? *(His voice breaking.)* Can you not see how your indifference wounds me sharper than any dagger? *(He turns Maria around toward him and clasps her hands in his).* Can you not see how much I am in love with you? And yet, you do not even grant me a glance? Each night, my heart weeps for yours! *(Weeping.)* I implore you, Maria, love me! For I will surely die of love if you do not feel what I do!

[He pulls her in to kiss her lips. Maria retracts, startled by his intensity. Alessandro perceives her withdrawal, just now realising the gravity of his words and the severity of his actions.]

MARIA

– partly in fear and partly perplexed. – Alessandro, please. You must not say such things to me again.

[Alessandro presses the back of his hand against his mouth in anguish.]

ALESSANDRO

– in shock and with a trembling voice. – Forgive me. I am tormented, Maria. I shall speak no more.

[Alessandro exits, his arms limp, his mouth slightly parted. His heart heaves, but no words come. He gazes at the ground, despondent. Maria watches him as he goes.]

MARIA

– saddened. – Holy Mary, Queen of Virgins... lend me thy strength. In thy heart were seven swords. In mine, one shall be enough.

[She bows her head in prayer and continues with her duties. The wind carries her prayer. The sky darkens faintly, though no storm comes. A stillness lingers.]

SCENE 4

It is the ninth day of the novena to the Queen of Virgins. The dwelling of Luigi and Assunta Goretti is filled with the light of candles and the soft murmurs of prayer, mingled with the uneasy breathing of Luigi. Around the bed stand Assunta and their five children; Giovanni stands close by. Alessandro lingers behind, partly in the shadows, his gaze fixed sorrowfully upon Maria. A silent dread and the anticipation of death hang in the air. A thousand worries race through the mind of Assunta. The priest, Father Raffaelo, enters silently, holding reverently the Holy Eucharist. All kneel in worship as he draws near.

FATHER RAFFAELO

– *solemnly, approaching the bedside.* – *In nomine Patris, et Filii, et Spiritus Sancti...* Luigi Goretti, receive now the Body of Christ, the food of pilgrims, the strength of the weak, the solace of the dying. Depart, my son, under the mantle of the Virgin's mercy.

[He administers the Eucharist. Luigi opens his eyes slightly, gazing upward as though beholding an unseen realm.]

LUIGI

– *faintly, dreamily.* – Look, the heavens open... fields of lilies and roses... pure as the dawn. Maria, daughter, you are clothed in light, crowned with gold. In your left hand, the lily of the valley. In your right hand, the branch of the palm... *(Gravely.)* But above are clouds of darkness, and shadows draw near you...

[Assunta grips Luigi's hand tightly, her voice trembling.]

ASSUNTA

– *withholding tears.* – Speak not of shadows in these moments, Luigi. Speak to us of your love, for behold, my tears, and those of your sons and daughters, fall upon you as rain upon the fields.

LUIGI

– *with tender firmness, voice weakening.* – Weep not for me, beloved. Weep for yourself and for our children. Assunta, heed me... return with haste to our former home in Gianturco. Shelter our children from the coming tempest that draws near you all with great wind.

ASSUNTA

– *anguished, voice breaking* – How shall I return, husband? We have nothing left but tears and prayers. Your sons are but boys, and are not yet men! What shall I do without you?

LUIGI

– *softly, yet resolutely.* – Better a crust of bread with peace, than plenty with darkness. *(Luigi lifts his hand, gently caressing Assunta's cheek.)* You are strong, Assunta. Your strength is greater than the mountains. Trust in the Virgin, and she shall guide you.

[Assunta begins weeping. Giovanni steps forward.]

GIOVANNI

– *humbly, with great sincerity.* – Be not troubled, my friend. God grant you rest. Forgive my weakness, that I could not save you.

LUIGI

– *gently smiling.* – Giovanni... you have been more brother than friend. Protect my family, I beg you...

[Alessandro steps forward hesitantly, his voice uncertain.]

ALESSANDRO

– *softly, awkwardly.* – Be at peace, Signore Goretti. Your family shall not be alone. I promise.

[Luigi's gaze briefly touches Alessandro. He says nothing, yet looks upon him gravely. He then rests his gaze upon Maria with profound sadness and love.]

LUIGI

Maria... beloved child...

MARIA

– *stepping closer, voice trembling with innocent sorrow.* – Papa...

LUIGI

– *voice growing faint, prophetic.* – Fear not, my Maria. In this, my final hour, God has granted me the insight of heaven. You shall overcome a great darkness, for a crown of glory awaits you. Not of this earth, but of heaven.

[He looks serenely beyond himself. For a moment, he speaks with the voice of a young man.]

LUIGI

– *clearly, yet softly.* – I go now to the land of eternal sunlight, where no famine, no toil, nor pain, nor tears exist. Only peace, my beloved ones. Eternal peace...

[His voice trails off. A deep serenity comes over his face. Giovanni steps forward, deeply moved. Luigi's eyes close gently. His breathing slows, and his hand falls softly. Silence overtakes the room. Assunta breaks into tears, holding Luigi's hand against her heart. The children weep gently. Father Raffaelo silently makes the Sign of the Cross over the body of Luigi.]

MARIA

– *quietly, kneeling and clasping her rosary, her teary eyes lifted heavenward.* – O Mary, Queen of Virgins, pray for us now, and at the hour of our death. Amen.

[All murmur softly, echoing her prayer. Outside, the wind rises mournfully, carrying the prayers upward. Alessandro stands apart, his gaze lingering on Maria, his face shadowed with a mixture of sorrow, longing, and fear. A flock of birds fly upward unto heaven, carrying the soul of Luigi.]

ACT II

SCENE 1

It is the dawn of Saturday, the 5th of July, 1902. The sun is still occult beneath the earth, but the aurora rises, pale and blue. Though the earth remains silently asleep, the Goretti family is wide awake and preparing for the day. Several oil lamps burn. Assunta, weary yet resolute, prepares herself, Mariano, and Sandrino for the day. Maria, sluggish and half-asleep, tends to Ersilia. Teresa remains asleep. Assunta notices Maria's marked fatigue and despondent demeanour.

ASSUNTA

– *hurriedly, but attentive.* – Maria, I see you as one who has worked a thousand days without rest. Your eyes are as the caverns and mines of the South, where men's eyes are dark and hollow as the Earth. Were you awake this night?

[Maria separates herself from Ersilia, signaling to her to continue alone, then walks toward her mother.]

MARIA

– *fatigued, yet anguished.* – Mother, this night, sleep has failed to come to me. Lovingly did I say my vespers, yet the peace of sleep did not fall upon me. My mind was ill at ease. Beyond the window did I hear the wind whisper my name throughout the night. The sky was dark and dreary and I found no solace in looking into it. It seemed to me as though the stars had concealed their light in fear. *(Embracing her mother, trembling with fear.)* How dark was the Earth last night, Mother, as it was the eve when Christ died. Though I closed my eyes, my mind troubled me, though I know not why – and continues yet!

ASSUNTA

– *empathetically.* – I have forgotten that you are still a girl. Nonetheless, eleven summers pass you now, and you must prepare to rid yourself of childish fears. There is much to do and you ought not to spend time entertaining such thoughts. You must be big now.

MARIA

– *looking up to her mother's eyes fearfully.* – But Mother, what I tell you are not the fears of Ersilia or Sandrino! When half the night's course had run, and the Earth was covered in a blanket of darkness and silence, I heard the *cucolo* cry! Truly do I tell you, Mother, that from that midnight hour onward, thrice did I hear the *cucolo* cry! *(Begins to desperately cry.)* You know well that his song is a hymn of danger and death!

[Assunta casts Maria aside and continues her preparations for the day. Maria continues crying.]

ASSUNTA

– *firmly, but with care.* – Maria, you must not allow those superstitions to bog your mind when you know there is much to do for the day. Cry no more, for these fears are merely the final fragments of your childhood that are still clinging desperately to existence within you. Soon, you will be a woman, and as myself, you will not have time to cry for such things. Come now, help me prepare breakfast.

[Maria prepares breakfast for her siblings. Assunta prepares breakfast for herself. A knock is suddenly heard at the door. Maria is startled. Assunta goes to open. Giovanni enters]

GIOVANNI

– *normally, with a happy tone.* – Good day, Assunta. And good day to you, Maria.

BOTH

– *in unison.* – Good day, Giovanni.

ASSUNTA

Where is your son?

GIOVANNI

He remains asleep in his chamber. I do not expect him to rise soon.

[Giovanni looks away, despondent. Assunta perceives his silence and grows curious.]

ASSUNTA

Is something the matter, Giovanni?

GIOVANNI

– *reservedly.* – No, Assunta, thank you. Only... *(He hesitates.)* Alessandro spent the entirety of the night in restlessness. Much did he toss and turn relentlessly. When I asked him what troubled him, he dismissed my concern. I think it may be, perhaps, a fever that has assailed him. For indeed, I saw him sweat much and remove his garments. He complained of the heat of summer and of an ardour in his chest. I know not how else to explain his behaviour for, as you know, the night was rather fair.

[Maria looks up discreetly, disturbed by the mention of Alessandro. She quickly resumes her duties.]

GIOVANNI

– *continuing.* – And last night, as I said my prayers ... *(Laughs nervously.)* The crucifix I have on the wall fell of its own accord. I know such things are of old women and the past, but I cannot help but hear my grandmother's voice in my head and grow nervous.

[Maria hears these words and becomes afraid. She runs to her mother, embracing her mother's legs with tears.]

MARIA

– *exclaiming* – Oh, Mother, do you see now the night that has passed over us? Stay, and do not leave me! Refrain from the fields and toil not today!

ASSUNTA

– *sternly.* – Enough, Maria! Be not ungrateful! The money is little, and the mouths to feed are many! Abandon your childish fears at once!

[She shakes Maria off. Then, turning to Giovanni...]

ASSUNTA

– *continuing.* – My apologies, Giovanni.

GIOVANNI

– *sympathetically.* – I meant not to scare her.

[Maria whimpers quietly to herself.]

ASSUNTA

– *calmly.* – You did no such thing. Children, rise and come. For yet another day of toilsome labour awaits us all.

SCENE 2

The chamber of Alessandro Serenelli, twenty years of age, in the dark twilight of early morning. Behind his bed, a single window is opened towards the silent mountains. Alessandro lies barely clothed, sweating and impassioned, upon a tangled bed. His skin is flushed, and his breath unsteady. A dim candle faintly illuminates the corner of the chamber. Evil spirits enter through the window from the mountains and surround him in the form of shadows. They float and loom about the entire room, encircling him as a fog. They whisper, in great numbers, all about him – yet only he can hear them. His eyes are dark and sleepless. A great and overwhelming storm of passion rises within him.

ALESSANDRO

– *with quiet frustration.* – Leave me be, leave me be! Cruel desire that has inflamed my heart and pierced it with arrows and swords! I have tossed about the night as the restless wind that circles endlessly in the dark night, yearning desperately to embrace the earth, yet finding no touch! From the crown of my head to the soles of my feet, penetrating even my entrails, this heat of desire encompasses me and drives me mad with thoughts of Maria! Within me rages a storm-cloud, gravid with rain, yet forbidden to release its waters upon the virgin earth!

[Alessandro wipes the sweat from his brow. The evil spirits giggle at his carnal frustration.]

ALESSANDRO

– *pleading.* – Tirelessly have you, evil spirits of the mountain, whispered in my ear alluring temptations! (*Louder.*) Endlessly have you filled my mind with passionate fantasies and dreams!

[The shadows swirl about more vividly, as if dancing and rejoicing in his passion. Alessandro looks about the room at the spirits' wicked dance.]

ALESSANDRO

– *with passionate tears.* – Why have you come, spirits of the mountain? Why do you pour in and out as a torrent of black water from the sea into my chamber? Even now, a great number surround me and bid me surrender unto my passion!

[The evil spirits cast visions of Maria and other forbidden passions before his eyes in the shadows of the room.]

ALESSANDRO

– *tenderly.* – Sweet, gentle, little lamb, purest among all the flock. Allow me to embrace you. Allow me to kiss your gentle head and caress your soft skin. Your hair flows as silken threads spun by the hands of angels and coloured with the olive tree! Your smile is fleeting and tender, as the first blossoms of spring. Maria, you fill me with longing and despair to keep you safe within my arms. I am your pilgrim, and you are my saint.

[He rises from his pallet, a sudden realisation coming upon him]

ALESSANDRO

– *softly, with clarity.* – The flesh is weak, but the spirit is willing... Depart, spirits of sinful desire! Return hence to the mountains! Go forth and flee to your abode within the coldness and darkness of the caverns! This is sin of both mind and flesh!

[The fog coalesces into a dark cloud and, as a river that runs in the blackness of the night, rushes out the window toward the mountains. As the last shadow flees the room, it leaves behind an article, purposefully dropping it. A silence pervades the room, leaving Alessandro alone with his thoughts and panting breaths. He walks toward the window where the sound of a dropped metal object was heard.

There, below the window, he finds an awl.]

ALESSANDRO

– *tiredly.* – Shadows of the mount and vale, why did you not depart in peace? (*He picks up the awl.)* What is this blade that shines in the darkness?

[He sees himself in the dim reflection of the blade.]

ALESSANDRO

– *with fatigue.* – Truly, this passion is greater than I can bear. For you are a lamb, Maria, and I, a ravenous wolf. When the wind carries the scent of your sweat and breath, it causes me to tremble. *(He touches the tip of the blade.)* Oh, cruel and tender heart, you shall never yearn for in me what I yearn for in you! *(Returning to passionate exclamations.)* I cannot abandon you! For if I do, then another shall come and have you for himself. In but a few years, a youth or shepherd shall play his flute, lure you into the meadows, and lay claim to that which I have long desired! *(He slams his fist against the pallet.)* No! It cannot be! Thus, in like manner that the rancher shears the fur of the lamb to preserve its beauty, so too shall I do with you, Maria. For I do swear, upon the Earth, the waters of the Earth, and the waters of the waters beneath the Earth, that if you cannot be mine, then you cannot belong to none.

[Alessandro looks resolutely toward the mountains, holding the awl firmly in his hand. The sun rises shamefully upon the land. The sky is as pale as the lips of a corpse. The morning bird does not dare sing. Above the fields, a vulture glides in circles.]

Why do you pour in and out as a torrent of black water from the sea!
Sweet, gentle, little lamb, purest among all the flock. Allow me to embrace you. Allow me to kiss your gentle head and caress your soft skin.
Spirits of sinful desire, return hence to the mountains!

SCENE 3

It is the early afternoon of the same day. The sun shines scorchingly in the midheaven. Giovanni, Assunta, Angelo (13), Mariano (9), Sandrino (7), and Ersilia (5) are working in the field. Maria has put the infant Teresa (3) to sleep. She wanders about the chamber in a state of unease. A nameless anxiety haunts her mind and spirit. The silence and solitude of the chamber suffocate her with thoughts and fears. She attempts to sew, yet her hands do not avail themselves. The thread slips from her fingers. She cannot still herself.

MARIA

– *overwhelmed.* – Oh heart, be at ease! Why do you disturb me? Thy beating is mightier than drums or an army of a thousand men! Oh, mind, why do you fill me with fears of nothing? I look about me and see monsters in the air where there are none! Oh, body, cease your trembling! You sway to and fro as the grain of the fields.

[A bird perched on the window flies eastward. The beating of its wings is loud, and frightens Maria. She lets out a gasp.]

MARIA

– *agonised.* – Ought I to go out to the fields? *(She steps outside the front door momentarily and gazes upon the distant fields where her mother and siblings labour arduously.)* No, I ought not. Look how they sweat and toil in the fields. It is true that the burdens are heavy and the money is light. *(She beholds the sleeping Teresa sorrowfully.)* This is the least I can do. Yes, I must abandon my fears and do what I must... For Mother... and Father.

[Maria reenters the chamber and resumes her duties. She takes a moment to breathe amidst the chores. All is still.]

MARIA

– *pensive.* – Such a silence...

[The birds are silent outside. The wind is mute and dormant. The sighs of the infant Teresa have ceased. Eternity passes in a moment. Alessandro enters through the inner door, disheveled. The sight of him causes Maria to step aback.]

MARIA

– *affrighted.* – Alessandro, your father is in the fields, and my mother is with him. There is none here with me besides my sister, if it is they whom you seek.

ALESSANDRO

– *minacious.* – I have not come seeking either my father or your mother. Rather, I have come seeking you.

[He walks toward Maria. With every step he takes, Maria steps slightly back, slowly drawing nearer to the outer door.]

MARIA

– *still with fear.* – And for what purpose?

ALESSANDRO

For many months have you withheld your affections from me, Maria, as the sun withholds its light from the night. You have been quite rude and not very loving with me.

[Maria perceives that he is unlike prior times, yet her innocence disables her from discerning his madness. Nevertheless, her inner wisdom intuits sagaciously.]

MARIA

– *placatingly.* – Alessandro, you make no sense. Tirelessly, despite your offenses, have I prayed for you. I have offered all my supplications to the thrones of the Seven Blessed Virgins—Cecilia, Lucia, Ursula, Barbara, Agatha, Agnes, and Anastasia—to all the angels of heaven, and to She who is Lady and Queen over them all, pleading that your soul may at last find peace. Do you think I have not seen your eyes, and how they appear as two dark moons in a starless night? See your hair, how it sways in wild disorder, as though stirred by winds of unrest. See the sweat upon your brow, how it pours down your face as though you laboured in the fields from dusk till dawn. I worry for you, because I love you, and I feel your soul walking upon a path of darkness.

[Maria's breaths grow more rapid. She begins to tremble. Alessandro draws closer.]

ALESSANDRO

– *unfazed.* – Indeed, Maria, my soul ventures ever closer towards the precipice of darkness. However, it follows a beautiful seven-rayed star that sings sweet songs and lures it in with lulling perfume. Yet, whenever my soul draws near to it, it flees ever farther. My soul has pursued this light even unto collapse, and now it falls into the sea of passion. Even now, I fall farther still, and yet, I do not swim, I drown.

[Alessandro presses her aggressively against the door. Maria whimpers.]

MARIA

– *struggling.* – Alessandro, what are you doing? Let me go!

[Alessandro caresses her cheek with the back of his index and middle finger. He hushes her, and whispers gently in her ear.]

ALESSANDRO

– *still gently.* – Why are you afraid of me? Do you not love me?

[His hand travels slowly down her arm.]

MARIA

– *oppressed.* – You confuse love with sin! No!

[She attempts to open the door to flee. He presses her arms more firmly against it.]

ALESSANDRO

Little lamb, you shall never flee from me. *(He kisses her slowly on the cheek. Maria begins to weep. He covers her mouth.)* Maria, unless you do what I am about to ask of you, I shall kill you.

[Maria looks pleadingly into his eyes, waiting for him to speak.]

ALESSANDRO

Before the lily wilts in the heat of June, the gardener must pluck it from the ground and harvest its beauty. And though its fragrance lasts only for a time, its sweetness is incomparable to any other flower. You are the lily, Maria, and I the gardener. I desire the flower of your purity and the sweetness thereof.

[Alessandro embraces her passionately. Maria manages to slip out from beneath him and push herself away. She runs in the opposite direction, toward the kitchen.]

MARIA

– *shouting and with fear.* – No! That is a mortal sin, and God does not want it! You shall go to hell, Alessandro! Cease! I do not love you like that!

[Alessandro is speechless, as if a thousand arrows have pierced his heart. He

beholds Maria with a gaze of pain and anguish. This gaze of heartbreak quickly transforms into one of anger and rage.]

ALESSANDRO
– *with fury.* – If you will not consecrate yourself to me, then no man shall be able to claim you as his own!

[Alessandro leaps toward her, pinning her to the ground. Maria is helpless beneath his bodyweight. His hands press against her throat, suffocating her. Her arms flail in the air, uselessly. Tears fall from the face of Alessandro and mingle with those of Maria. Maria manages to inhale quickly.]

MARIA
– *barely breathing.* – I would rather die before committing sin and offending God, for the purity of my youth belongs to Him alone!

ALESSANDRO
– *with tears and frustration.* – So be it! If your heart shall not beat for me, then may it cease to beat, and mine with it! If your body shall not surrender itself unto me, then let it be undone, and my soul with it! Sinful eyes, behold your final delight!

[Alessandro takes out the awl and stabs Maria nine times. Alessandro stabs Maria so intensely, the blade pierces her body six times. The final three strike her spine. Alessandro beholds Maria, unconscious, and believes her to be dead. He weeps over her body, embracing her.]

ALESSANDRO
– *sobbing.* – Even death cannot mar her beauty. Indeed, she lies not dead, rather, asleep.

[The heat of passion settles, and the realisation of his crime dawns upon him

dreadfully. He rises and beholds the slain victim, who lies gracefully on the floor while her blood pools around her, as a lily among roses. His eyes widen, and he begins breathing intensely. A paranoiac dread besieges him.]

ALESSANDRO

– *in overwhelming shock.* – My iniquity is greater than I can bear! I retreat, for he that finds me shall surely slay me! *(He lifts the awl to his face and beholds himself in the sullied reflection of the blade.)* Sinful creature, vagabond of creation, you are now a guilty fugitive! Retreat, and hide your face in shame!

[Alessandro runs madly into his inner chamber. Some time passes. He hears a stir in the main chamber. Rising, he goes hence and sees Maria dragging herself toward the door. A pool of crimson trails behind her. She manages to unlock the latch and reaches to open the door. Mistaking the sight for a vision, imagining that she has risen from the dead to curse him, Alessandro rushes toward her. He throws her once again to the ground and stabs her five more times. He retreats once again to his inner chamber, dropping the bent blade onto the floor. Maria regains consciousness momentarily, as the last light of day that surrenders itself unto the twilight.]

MARIA

– *dying.* – "Forgive us our sins... Powerful Virgin, merciful Virgin, faithful Virgin."

[Maria collapses into unconsciousness. Her blood continues to usher forth from her body. The infant Teresa begins to cry aloud, as if mourning the assault upon her sister. Her cries fade as a distant echo.]

SCENE 4

The lower chamber of the Goretti farmhouse. Two hours have passed since the assault. Clouds begin to draw nigh upon the land. Giovanni returns from the fields, dazed by the heat of the summer sun. A wooden bench bears the weight of his midsummer dream and the stupor of his siesta. The house lies still – until a scream shatters the silence.

MARIA

– *a weak cry aloud.* – Mama! Help me!

[With a sudden jolt of dread, Giovanni rises, dazed and disoriented. He stumbles up the stairway as he rushes upstairs. There, he finds Maria in a pool of blood, injured, and fading between consciousness. The infant Teresa begins wailing. Instinctively, he shouts from the height of the landing toward the fields, where Assunta and her children toil. Assunta's maternal instincts unhesitatingly impel her to run towards the farmhouse. Her children run with her. Giovanni crouches beside Maria, lifting her head and touching her brow. Her skin is fevered and straining toward death.]

GIOVANNI

– *desperately.* – Who has done this to you, Maria?

[Maria's eyes open and close weakly, burdened by pain.]

MARIA

– *moaning, weak, and in anguish.* – ...Alessandro.

[She fades back into unconsciousness as quickly as she regained it. Giovanni is

baffled by her response. Assunta and her other children arrive at the scene. All are horrified and begin to wail. Assunta commands Angelo to call the Carabinieri. Angelo obeys and dashes out. Assunta descends and embraces her assailed daughter. Maria's blood stains her face and hands. Giovanni remains silent and weeping.]

ASSUNTA

– *in despair.* – Oh, my daughter, forgive me! Blood of my blood, flesh of my flesh, only today did I have you in my arms alive, and now I have you at the point of death. *(Caressing Maria's face.)* Tender face which I so often kissed and held. The blood which at once flushed upon your cheeks now pours out as a stream. Oh, could I but give you all the blood within my body now! *(Kissing her closed eyelids.)* Little eyes which I so often kissed and beheld myself within, now your light fades away and retracts as the sun behind the clouds. Oh, could I but give you my eyes now! *(Lifting her head upward in sorrow.)* Lord and Lady of Heaven, to whom all things are made known, though I, a miserable sinner, know not thy wondrous designs and purposes – I offer unto thee my daughter, that she may be thine. Blessed art thou, O Virgin, who stood beneath the cross, and watched thy innocent child bleed for the world. *(She gasps strongly, tears streaming endlessly. Then, speaking as though swearing a vow.)* Now, O Queen, unto thee I too give mine own. Virgin of Sorrows, here lieth before thy throne thy daughter. As thou didst offer the fruit of thy womb for the salvation of the world, so too do I set upon thy altar the fruit of my womb, that she may be as incense before thee and thy Son, and her blood as wine pressed from the vine of innocence, and her pure flesh broken as bread. Unto thee alone, O Virgin, do I surrender thy daughter.

[After a time of incessant, speechless tears, from the bottom of the stairs are heard heavy footsteps that dash quickly upward. The Carabinieri have come.]

CARABINIERI

– *authoritatively.* – Where is the assailant!

[Giovanni, shamefully and with many tears, signals toward the inner chamber. The police find Alessandro and take him away, along with Giovanni for interrogation. Four hours transpire until the horse-drawn medical carriage arrives. The medics carry Maria's body and place it delicately in the cart. The blood of Maria Goretti falls upon the ground as she is carried away. The Earth receives the drops of her innocent blood which cry out unto God. The seven virgins weep from heaven, their tears pour down as gentle summer rain upon the land.]

"The seven virgins weep from heaven, their tears pour down as gentle summer rain upon the land."

The Passion of St. Maria Goretti, Act II.

SCENE 5

It is The Hour of Great Mercy on Sunday, July 6th. Maria lieth in a hospital bed in Nettuno, Lazio, her mother beside her. She has undergone surgery without anesthesia and endures agonising pain. A thousand thoughts and regrets haunt the mind of Assunta. Assunta tearfully clasps the weak hand of her daughter. About the air hangs a subtle, gentle light, perceptible only to Maria. Beside her bed, a window faces the western sky. On the wall opposite the sick bed hangs a portrait of the Blessed Virgin and the Divine Child.

MARIA
– *gently.* – Mother... *(Licking her dry, pale lips.)* I thirst.

[Assunta calls politely for a nurse. She quickly arrives.]

ASSUNTA
– *graciously, concealing her tears.* – May my daughter have a drink of water?

[The nurse glances through several sheets of paper on a table in the corner of the room.]

NURSE
Allow me to speak with the doctor. I shall bring him at once.

[The nurse politely dismisses herself. Assunta caresses the forehead of her daughter, gently removing a strand of hair from her face.]

ASSUNTA
– *sorrowful and with regret.* – Maria, forgive me. The only one to blame here is me. It was I who ought to have been in the home. It was I who ought to have

been a mother to your siblings – not you.

MARIA
– *with a fragile, gentle smile* – It was God's will.

ASSUNTA
– *with tears* – Forgive me... Forgive that I could not be there, where you are instead.

[She places her head gently upon Maria's chest, weeping. Maria kisses Assunta's forehead.]

MARIA
It was God's will.

ASSUNTA
Oh my God, give unto me all the pain that my daughter feels. Allow me to feel it in her place! Allow me to take it into myself! Could I not lie here instead of her?

[Maria directs her gaze toward the painting of Mary and Christ on the wall.]

MARIA
It was God's will.

[Amidst heavy weeping, the sound of heavy footsteps upon the floor is heard drawing nigh.]

MARIA
– *solemnly.* – Look, Mother, the messenger approaches. The proclamation of my end walks upon the floorboards. Let it be done unto me according to what was willed from before my birth.

[Assunta wonders at the significance of these words. The Doctor enters.]

DOCTOR

Hello, my child. The nurse has informed me of your thirst.

[He speaks with both strength of voice and kindness. Assunta looks at the doctor with an imploring expression. His gaze meets hers, grave and heavy.]

DOCTOR

– *reservedly.* – I lament this news, but it cannot be done. (*He looks upon Assunta with pitiful eyes.)* It is a miracle your daughter even still draws breath... Her fourteen perforations have punctured her intestines and caused an infection of the abdomen. Whatever she ingests will flow out from within her.

[Assunta throws herself out upon the foot of the bed.]

ASSUNTA

– *helplessly.* – Oh, daughter, could I but give you all the tears of my life as refreshment! I shed them all now for you!

[She embraces her daughter in sorrow and shame. The Doctor takes a deep breath before speaking further.]

DOCTOR

I lament that my regret ends not there... I am sorry... Our operation was unsuccessful in mitigating the infection. Maria bleeds from within her body and draws near the point of death.

[Assunta gasps, as if her very soul escaped from her mouth. Maria, however, continues with unwavering tranquility.]

MARIA

– *peacefully.* – Weep no more, Mother. For heaven has already told me what this man has said here on Earth. The hour of my departure has come.

[The Doctor marvels at her words. He silently dismisses himself. A single tear falls quietly onto the floor from his eyes. The heart of Assunta breaks into a thousand pieces. Maria preserveres in grace and serenity.]

MARIA

Shall we spend my final moments here on Earth in sorrow, Mother? I implore you, weep no more, for it weighs heavily upon my soul. Be joyous now, for God has not forgotten me. He has, in his benevolence, granted that I shall not leave this earthly plane without having taken the Bread of Life. In but a few moments, he shall send me one to impart upon me the final sacrament, for the Good Shepherd abandons not his sheep in time of need.

[Assunta ceases her lamentation and weeps from within. She spends some time alone with Maria, embraced. A while after, Father Raffaello enters. He beholds the dying Maria and the grieving Assunta. In one hand he holds a miniature tabernacle. In the other, a vessel of blessed oil. He places both on the desk beside Maria.]

FATHER RAFFAELLO

– *in dismay.* – Assunta... Maria, child. I came as quickly as I could.

[He walks to the side of the bed. He holds Maria gently by her hand. Assunta is comforted by his familiar presence.]

FATHER RAFFAELLO

– *gently.* – Do you remember me?

MARIA

– *with a soft, yet weak happiness.* – Yes, I do. I knew you would come, for your angel had come and told me.

[All marvel at her response.]

FATHER RAFFAELLO

– *sublimating his surprise.* – Then you know what I have come to do, and for what purpose?

[Maria quietly nods.]

MARIA

To quench the thirst of my soul and grant me the food of pilgrims. For though my body thirsts, my soul shall be refreshed by the living bread. Indeed, I have begged for water, and none have given me any.

FATHER RAFFAELLO

– *a sense of understanding comes upon him.* – Maria, Christ our Lord also, from the cross, begged for water and none gave Him any. Will you likewise offer up your thirst and pain for sinners?

[Maria quietly nods. Assunta steps aside so that Father Raffaello may perform the final sacrament. He places a crucifix upon Maria's chest. She holds it close to her heart, lovingly. He takes the vessel of oil and anoints her forehead with it.]

FATHER RAFFAELLO

– *solemnly.* – With this sacred anointing, may the Bridegroom of souls prepare thee for thy wedding to eternity. May the dew of His mercy fall upon thy lips, and His Spirit enter thee as incense fills the temple. He who breaks the seal of death shall lift thee as a lily from the soil of the earth, and crown thee in the gardens of His light as a seal upon His sacred heart.

[He then takes the miniature tabernacle into his hands and reverently administers the Eucharist. All seems to become brighter. Maria gazes at the host adoringly.]

FATHER RAFFAELLO

– *Holding up the Body of Christ before Maria.* – Whoso eateth my flesh and drinketh my blood shall not perish, but have eternal life.

[Maria consumes the host. All pain within her seems to fade away. Suddenly, she regains her former strength of voice. Her countenance transitions from the paleness of death to a sudden luminosity. Both Assunta and Father Raffaello are taken aback. Assunta takes hold of one hand and Father Raffaello of the other. Maria's gaze is directed once again to the portrait of Mary upon the wall, as if looking beyond it. Assunta and Father Raffaello are reminded of Luigi's final moments.]

MARIA

– *peaceful and clear.* – Mother, Father, I see a woman before me. How beautiful is she! She has skin as white as the purest clouds, and eyes as blue as the morning sky. Upon her head rests a crown of stars. She extends to me a crown of gold. Before I am taken away to go with her, I shall say one final thing: Let it be known in Heaven and on the Earth that, for the love of Christ the Lord, I forgive Alessandro Serenelli for his sin, and I want him with me in heaven for eternity.

[Maria smiles and releases a gentle sigh. Her soul ascends to heaven and takes its place in the throne room of the Queen of Heaven, among the choir of Celestial Virgins and Princesses. In her right hand is placed a lily, and in her left, the branch of the palm. On her finger, the ring of her betrothal to Christ, the Bridegroom.]

ACT III

SCENE 1

It is the early morning of Good Friday, 1910. In the prison chamber of solitary confinement, where Alessandro Serenelli is enchained by the ankle. The earth is veiled in the final hour of darkness before dawn. It is the hour in which the Lord was condemned. The prison chamber is dark and dreary, lit only by the faint light of the waning crescent moon, itself shrouded by heavy clouds. The dim light of the night seeps into his prison cell through a single, miniature square window, no greater than the size of a hand. Alessandro raves in his cell with madness and fury. Infernal spirits torment him with rage. He clutches and tosses his chains. Abominable and horrific visions swirl about. The air is thick with hostility and unseen taunting voices.

ALESSANDRO

– *with anger.* – Cursed spirits from the abyss! I curse you and your abode, which you have now made my skull, and my cell your place of torment! There is no rest for me, neither day nor night. About me flame the souls of the damned, who bid me join their underworld choir!

[He looks about the walls – horrified and mad, beholding terrible visions of infernal monsters.]

ALESSANDRO

– *frenzied.* – This prison shall be my tomb! The six-headed serpents of hell have come from their thorny nests in the skeletal trees! Listen to how they hiss and threaten me! And how the locusts from beneath the earth rear their pointed tails towards me! Why do you tarry, God of Punishment? Let my soul be food for hell! Let the worms begin their feast!

[Shadowy faces of demons appear before him in a cloud of black smoke, ready to consume him.]

ALESSANDRO

– *surrendering himself unto the shadows.*– Come and take your slave, bornless ones! Relieve me of my suffering! For that sin I shall pay – the slaying of the lamb. Oh, how many times have I seen her roaming the corridors in the prison of my mind? Even now, her memory returns as it were... pleading... innocent... Oh, it is an eternal shame that plagues me! How dare I ever mention your sweet name – that name which is above all names? Forgive me? How could you? Oh... Maria.

[As soon as he pronounces her name, a brilliant, dazzling light suddenly flashes in the air before him. The shadows flee, and the visions vanish. The regal figure of Maria appears within the light. She is radiant and fair. Alessandro sinks to the floor, concealing his face in shame and fear.]

ALESSANDRO

– *with pitiable fear, as a child.* – My reckoning has come! Little one, have you come from the heights of heaven to call down consuming fire? Let it be done! Let the fire fall upon me! But I beg you, do not approach me! *(Beholding her briefly as she draws near.)* No! Not this way! Look not upon me! Oh God, why does she come closer? Why does she look upon me with a silent smile? Her silence thunders louder than the trumpets of the archangels! Back, Back! Oh fire of heaven, rend me now! May her fingers become thunderbolts! May the earth open from beneath me and consume me, before your gaze, oh Maria, shatters me!

[With a gentle smile, Maria reveals a bundle of lilies beneath her arm. With gentility, she lets fall upon him fourteen lilies. Each one lands upon the skin of Alessandro and is consumed by a flame.]

ALESSANDRO

– *with a sudden sense of peace and awe.* – Each petal... a flame that purges my soul.

[Slowly, he braves himself to look upon her. She stands silent and still. There are no flames nor swords. Only inconceivable peace.]

ALESSANDRO

– *with tears of contrition and salvation.* – She does not smite, nor does she curse... She forgives. *(He kneels upright.)* You extend to me lilies, pure as yourself, and white as your soul. One by one, you let them fall upon me and forgive me of my sin. Fourteen sins did I commit against your flesh, fourteen lilies you let fall upon mine.

[He collapses forward and lies prostrate before Maria, sobbing.]

ALESSANDRO

Maria, Daughter of Light, Lily of the Marshes... Once, I saw you bleed till life had gone forth from you. And now, I see you crowned in light and adorned as one of the celestial princesses. Saint of God, Little Angel, guide me where I walk, that when I die, I may merit to stand at the farthest corner of heaven, to catch only a glimpse of you, seated among the virgins and angels. *(With divine surrender and trust.)* By the mercy of the Eternal, I have not been consumed, for His forgiveness blooms anew with the dawn. Each morning, His faithfulness rises with the sun, and sets not, though all things fade and fall. For from the abyss and this vale of tears have I cried unto Thee, O Lord, and thou hast mercifully inclined Thy ear to me. For if Thou, O Just Judge, should mark sin, who, O Lord, could stand? Yet, in Thee lies forgiveness, that men, beholding Thee, might tremble not of fear, but of love. O, God, who sittest upon Thy throne of mercy, purge me with hyssop, and I shall be made clean. I wish no longer to be myself, but rather, a vessel. For it is Christ who shall dwell within me. Once I was blind, but now I see the light of the Morning Star. Henceforth, I shall dwell in the house of the Lord. All the days of my life shall be as a censer before His altar. And I—yes, I, the sinner—shall behold the beauty of His face ... and Hers.

[He rises from his prostrate position... only to see the cell around him in silence. Maria is gone, but her peace remains. The scent of lilies lingers faintly in the air. He lifts his face gently toward the faint glow of morning. Outside, the morning star ascends in the east. The Dark Night of the Soul has passed. The dawn of the Day of Mercy has begun.]

"Maria, Daughter of Light, Lily of the Marshes..."

The Passion of St. Maria Goretti, Act III.

SCENE 2

It is the Third Hour of Good Friday. Distant processions can be heard from Alessandro's cell. He kneels in silent, contemplative prayer, facing the eastern window. Bolts and latches of the prison are heard being undone. The voices of the guards are heard speaking humbly. Soon, footsteps are heard approaching his cell.

ALESSANDRO
– *shouting informatively, still facing away from the entrance.* – If you have brought me food to eat, I ask you to give it to another and let it not be for waste. For today the Lord has been crucified for our sins, and I offer my hunger as penance.

A VOICE FROM WITHOUT
The peace of God, Alessandro. Greetings.

[Alessandro turns around and sees Father Raffaello standing before him. He remains silent for a moment, mistaking him for another vision.]

FATHER RAFFAELLO
– *puzzled.* – Are you well?

[Alessandro rises, realising he is speaking with flesh and bone.]

ALESSANDRO
– *surprised, yet serene.* – Peace be with you, Father. *(Taking a moment to observe him.)* You are familiar to me...

[Alessandro recalls the eve Luigi died.]

ALESSANDRO

Ah, yes! You were there in Le Ferriere to administer the final sacrament to Luigi. May he rest in peace.

FATHER RAFFAELLO

Indeed... and I was also there to administer the final sacrament to Maria.

[Alessandro beholds him with a gaze of faith.]

ALESSANDRO

Father, why have you come?

FATHER RAFFAELLO

– *introspectively.* – Eight years have passed since the departure of Maria from her earthly life. Since then, devotion to her has spread throughout the countryside. Her intercession is implored amongst the people, and miracles occur in her name. And now, the Holy See receives petitions from the devout, that she may be numbered among the communion of saints. I came to share this grace with you, that even from suffering and tragedy, God brings forth light.

ALESSANDRO

– *beholding Father Raffaello with a gaze full of peace and divine clarity, speaking with a voice as if from another life.* – Ah, so that was it... Yes, yes, I now know, I now see.... Before your coming, I was not conscious; but now I see it was bound to be. This earth is no longer the same earth. I have come to know, by that light which came from above, that it is through pain that God fashions His saints – those blessed ones whom He sets apart and calls to suffer, that some greater light might pass through them into the world. I raise my eyes to the heaven of light and see the mercy of God envelop the world!

[Alessandro falls before Father Raffaello, kneeling before him supplicatingly. He tenderly takes the priest's hand into his own, and presses it close against his face.]

ALESSANDRO

– *with profound penitence and a contrite heart.* – O my God, infinite in mercy and beauty, I have sinned against Thee, and before the faces of Thy angels and archangels, and beneath the eyes of Thy saints and virgins. With these hands have I defiled innocence, and with these eyes did I sin against purity. Yet still, Thou hast not abandoned me. O Sacred Heart, pierced for my transgression; O Virgin, whose heart compassioned me and did not smite me – I repent. I repent not only for the fear of judgment, but because I have pierced Love and Mercy itself. Have mercy on me, O Lord. Forgive me, for the sake of Her whose blood was mingled with Thine in martyrdom. Before Thy shepherd Raffaello do I vow to sin no more. Let me live and die as one who was broken, and remade in Thee. Amen!

FATHER RAFFAELLO

– *laying his hand gently upon Alessandro's head* – *In nomine Patris, et Filii, et Spiritus Sancti,* Alessandro Serenelli, son of Giovanni Serenelli, *ego te absolvo.* In the name of Him whose flesh thou pierced in hers, be washed and made anew. May peace envelop thee, and sin no more.

ALESSANDRO

– *with penitent, grateful tears.* – What shall be my penance?

FATHER RAFFAELLO

– *tenderly.* – You have wept, not as Cain, but rather, as Saint Peter. You have shown true repentance... and for true repentance, there must be true penance. But true penance is not imposed, it is chosen. *(Lifting his face up gently.)* Choose then, my son, your holy task. May your hands, once instruments of destruction, become instruments of mercy.

[The morning sun pours through the narrow window, bathing the cell in a golden hue.]

ALESSANDRO

Then may these hands, once bestial, now tend the wounds of the leper and feed the bread of the poor. I shall go where the olive groves are enveloped in mist, where the hills cradle silence, and the roses bloom in shade. Let no bell ring for me but that which tolls at matins; let no robe clothe me but that which the humble wear in silent prayer. There shall I pass among forgotten vineyards, and speak to stones and sparrows. My friends shall be the rosebush and the honeybee. I shall ask no more of life than the turning of a page in a psalter. For if the wind ought to carry my prayer, then may it carry me to where the barefoot man walks westward in the shadow of the Cross, and learns what it is to be poor and hidden. For even the lilies of the vale, in their white raiments, grow not proud in the sun, but bow reverently toward the tabernacle of the dawn... And so shall I.

FATHER RAFFAELLO

In the mountains of Marche, near the Sibyllines, there lies upon a hill a town by the name of Macerata. Once your time of imprisonment is complete, make your way to the Convent of San Lorenzo. Once arrived, ask for a man by the name of Vincenzo di Francesco. Tell him I have sent you, and he shall instruct you in the ways of God, where men walk westward in the shadow of the Cross, and learn what it is to be poor and hidden.

ALESSANDRO

Let it be done to me according to your word.

FATHER RAFFAELLO

Behold, Mercy and truth have met; righteousness and peace have kissed. Where sin once abounded, grace has abounded all the more. For He suffered for our sins, and by His suffering, we are forgiven. Now, my son, take up your cross and follow him. For in that path of suffering lies the road to eternal life. May the world remember not the sin that wrought the pain, but the pain that forgave the sin. For howsoever great may be one's agony, greater yet is the mercy that redeems it.

[Father Raffaello hands him a devotional prayer card of Maria Goretti, made by the country folk. On the face of the card, a painting of Maria Goretti holding a lily and a palm. Behind, the words of Christ: "Forgive, and thou shalt be forgiven."]

FIN

Bryan de Justin.